The Boxcar Children Mysteries

THE MYSTERY IN THE
OLD ATTIC

THE MYSTERY IN THE OLD ATTIC

created by
GERTRUDE CHANDLER WARNER

Illustrated by Charles Tang

SCHOLASTIC INC.
New York Toronto London Auckland Sydney

Activities by Nancy E. Krulik
Activity illustrations by Alfred Giuliani

ISBN 0-590-95598-5

12 11 10 9 8 7 6 5 4 3 2 1   7 8 9/9 0 1 2/0

Printed in the U.S.A.   40

First Scholastic printing, October 1997

Contents

CHAPTER 1

The Long Trip

"Watch, let go! I have to take these boots with me to Michigan," said six-year-old Benny as he tugged one end of his red snow boot.

Watch wagged his tail and obediently dropped the boot before scampering down the hallway to Jessie's room. There he began to sniff her open suitcase. "Watch, what are you doing?" said Jessie, laughing. She packed her thick white sweater and gently nudged her dog away.

"I think he wants to go with us," said

Violet as she came into Jessie's room carrying her purple ski jacket. Purple was Violet's favorite color, and she liked most of her clothes to be purple or lavender. "Do you think I will need this jacket and my wool coat, too?" Violet asked her older sister.

"No, probably just the jacket and one wool sweater," answered Jessie. "And don't forget your boots. Grandfather says it snows a lot in that part of Michigan."

Jessie, who was twelve years old, sometimes acted like a mother to her ten-year-old sister, Violet, and their two brothers, Henry, age fourteen, and Benny.

The children's parents had died when the children were younger, and Henry, Jessie, Violet, and Benny now had a home with their grandfather, James Alden, and his housekeeper, Mrs. McGregor. Even so, the Aldens were used to taking care of themselves. Just after their parents died, the children had lived all by themselves in a boxcar in the woods. Now the boxcar had a home, too — in Grandfather's backyard. The children often used the boxcar as a playhouse.

"Jessie, I can't wait to play in all that snow," said Benny as he ran into Jessie's room carrying his pink cup and a wool scarf. "I don't have room for these things in my suitcase. Can you take them?" he asked his sister.

"Sure, Benny," answered Jessie. Benny had had that pink cup ever since his boxcar days. He liked to take it with him wherever he went. Jessie carefully wrapped the scarf around the cup and put it in her suitcase. "Come on, Benny, I'll help you pack."

The next day the four Alden children and their grandfather were going to board a plane bound for Michigan's Upper Peninsula. Grandfather's aunt Sophie had died recently, and Grandfather had inherited her big old house, which he planned to sell. The children were traveling with him to help him clear it out.

"Jessie, did you know that Great-aunt Sophie's house is more than one hundred years old?" Benny asked.

Jessie nodded as she took a pair of roller skates out of Benny's suitcase to make room for his sweaters. "Yes, I know. And it's so big, it even has a ballroom in it."

Benny gulped. "That means we're going to have a lot of rooms to clean," he said.

The next morning, Watch ran around the car as the Aldens loaded all their suitcases into the trunk.

"Oh, Watch, I wish you could come, too," said Benny as he wrapped his arms around his dog's neck.

"He wouldn't like the long plane trip," Grandfather said gently.

Henry nodded. "It's true, Watch. Do you know we have to take two planes? One from Boston to Detroit. Then another from Detroit to Brockton, where Great-aunt Sophie's house is. And you would not even be allowed to ride with us."

Watch licked Henry's hands. Then Benny, Jessie, and Violet all took turns hugging their dog. Only then did Watch follow Mrs. McGregor up the steps to the front door.

"Good-bye," the Aldens called as Grandfather backed the car out of the driveway. "We'll write!" Jessie promised.

"Don't forget to wear your boots," Mrs. McGregor called.

"Boy, airports sure are crowded," said Benny as he followed his family to the waiting area at the gate. All the chairs were taken, so the Aldens went over to the window, where they could see the planes take off and land.

"Look, Benny, we'll probably be on a big jet like that," said Henry. He pointed to the Boeing 737 that was speeding down the runway. "But when we change in Detroit, we'll be on a puddle jumper."

"A what?" asked Benny.

"He means a very small plane that only carries about twenty or thirty people," Jessie explained.

"Oh," said Benny.

"Flight 131 is ready for boarding," an announcer spoke into a microphone.

"That's us. That's our flight." Henry sounded very excited.

* * *

Benny had a seat next to the window right near Grandfather. Violet, Jessie, and Henry were on the other side of the aisle. When the plane was high in the air, the flight attendant announced it would be all right to move around the cabin.

"Thank goodness. I need to stretch my legs," said Jessie.

"When is lunch?" asked Benny as he crossed the aisle to stand by Henry's seat.

Grandfather said, "You may have to be patient, Benny. The flight attendants have a lot of people to serve on this flight."

"Here, Benny, I'll show you where we're going," said Henry as he unfolded one of the many maps he carried in his jacket. "We're flying over these states," he continued as he traced a line with his finger over Massachusetts and New York. "Here is Detroit." Henry pointed to the city in the southern part of Michigan. "From there we'll catch a small plane and fly over the rest of Michigan and Wisconsin."

"We're going to the part of Michigan

that looks like a shoe," said Benny.

"Right," said Henry.

Benny sat down and tried to concentrate on the map Henry had given him. But his stomach was rumbling. "Grandfather," he said, poking James Alden in the arm. "Can you tell me again about Great-aunt Sophie and her big house in Michigan?"

"Of course, Benny." Grandfather liked telling the story almost as much as his grandchildren liked hearing it. "When I was a boy about your age, my parents would take me to the Upper Peninsula of Michigan almost every summer. We would always stay with Aunt Sophie in her big house near the lake."

"You mean Lake Superior," said Benny. He noticed that Grandfather had changed part of one of his favorite stories.

"Yes. Lake Superior," said Grandfather. "When my other cousins visited, they would stay in the big house, too. We would try to spend as much time outside as we could: fishing, camping, and visiting the copper mines."

"Copper mines?" Benny interrupted.

"Yes, the Upper Peninsula used to be filled with working copper mines. Most of them have been shut down now."

"Oh." Benny sounded disappointed.

"Anyway," Grandfather continued, "when it rained and we had to stay indoors, we would explore the old house. One summer we found a hidden passageway that connected the library to the attic, and another time we found a secret closet off the kitchen."

"What was in the secret closet?" asked Benny, even though he knew the answer.

"Oh, old snowshoes — and some very old toys that had belonged to my father. We found an old model sailboat and a beautiful rocking horse that my uncle had carved out of wood for his children."

Benny smiled. "I can't wait to explore the old house. I'm sure we'll find something exciting there."

Grandfather chuckled. "You probably will, Benny."

"Grandfather?" asked Violet from across the narrow aisle. "How come you never visited Aunt Sophie's house after you were eighteen?"

"Well," answered Grandfather, "Aunt Sophie started coming down to visit my family more often. And at eighteen, I started college and worked during the summers, so I did not have as much time to make that long trip anymore."

Violet was quiet. She knew how much Grandfather had enjoyed his summers in Michigan.

"I can't tell you how much I'm looking forward to showing you the Upper Peninsula," Grandfather said as he reached across the aisle to pat Violet on the arm. "There is no place as pretty, except for maybe Greenfield."

Violet laughed.

"Oh, lunch is here," said Benny happily as the flight attendant put a tray of chicken salad, bread, cheese, and a cookie in front of him.

"Mmm," said Benny.

CHAPTER 2

The Old House

Four hours later, the Aldens were in the little plane headed for Brockton's airport. Benny and Jessie could not stop looking out the window. All they could see were pine trees that stretched for miles before ending at the shores of a big blue body of water.

"That must be Lake Superior," said Benny.

Grandfather nodded. He was looking out the window, too, over Benny's shoulder. "It's just the way I remember it. Trees, trees, and more trees," he said, sounding very pleased.

"How come it's not snowing?" asked Benny.

Grandfather chuckled. "Don't worry, Benny. It will. There is usually snow on the ground five months of the year up here — from November to April."

It was late afternoon when Grandfather's rental car pulled into the circular driveway in front of Aunt Sophie's mansion. Sagging steps led up to a wide porch that went all around the mansion. Painted a mustard yellow with white trim, the house had big dormer windows, two towers, eight chimneys, and a big brass knocker on the front door.

"Wow," said Benny, bounding up the steps. "I've never seen a house like this. Can I have one of the tower rooms?"

Grandfather shook his head. "The top floor of the house is rented. When Aunt Sophie grew older, the house became too much for her, so she converted the top floor into apartments."

"Oh," said Benny. "The renters have the tower rooms?"

Grandfather nodded. "But you will have your choice of bedrooms. As I remember, there are at least five on the second floor."

"How many renters are there, Grandfather?" Jessie wanted to know.

"Two. One in each little apartment."

"Nothing about this house looks little," said Henry, shaking his head. "Look at those big trees in back." He pointed to some massive oaks.

Grandfather turned his key in the lock. "Let's go inside now."

The wooden door creaked open. The Aldens walked through a large parlor, then into the biggest living room the children had ever seen. A large crystal chandelier hung from the ceiling. Oriental rugs covered the parquet floors. A grand piano stood near the bay window, and scattered around the room were overstuffed armchairs, comfortable couches, and antique tables and chairs.

"Look at that fireplace," said Benny.

"It's big enough for me to sit in."

"I would not try that," said a strange voice.

The Aldens whirled around to face a middle-aged, balding man with a mustache and glasses. The man introduced himself to Grandfather. "Hello, I am Professor Francis Schmidt. I live upstairs on the third floor."

"Oh, yes," said Grandfather, shaking the man's hand. "You teach history at the local college. Aunt Sophie told me about you."

The professor nodded a little sadly. "Your aunt was a lovely woman," he said. He turned to look at Henry, Jessie, Violet, and Benny but did not say anything to them. He looked only at Grandfather when he spoke. "So, how long will you be staying?" he asked.

"Long enough to clean up the house a bit in order to sell it," answered Grandfather.

"I was afraid you might sell this old house, but I don't blame you. It would be a lot to take care of, especially when you don't live here."

"Yes," agreed Grandfather. "I do hate to sell it, though. I have so many fond memories of all the times I spent here as a boy. The house is very much the way I remember it."

The professor chuckled. "Your aunt was not one to change much. In all the years I've been renting, I've never even seen her move a stick of furniture from its usual place."

"No, that was not Aunt Sophie's way," said Grandfather. "She wanted the house to stay the same. After all, it was the house she had lived in most of her life."

"Well, if you'll excuse me, I must go back to grading papers," the professor said. "I have my own entrance to the house, so I will not be disturbing you. I just came in to introduce myself when I heard your voices."

"It was good to meet you," said Grandfather.

The professor turned to look pointedly at Benny. He cleared his throat before speaking. "I often work at home." The professor paused for effect. "So I do hope you children will not be too noisy. I do not wish to be disturbed when I am doing my research. Good day."

With that, the professor turned and walked out of the room. The children could hear his heavy footsteps on the stairs.

Benny frowned. "I am not noisy," he whispered.

Grandfather shrugged. "He probably isn't used to children," he said. "Anyhow, he won't be able to hear much of anything from the third floor. This house has very strong floors and walls. There's no need to whisper. In fact, he probably would not even hear the piano if we started playing." The children laughed.

"Come on. Let's explore some more," said Benny. He forgot how tired he was after the long plane trip. "I want to see the secret closet."

"Yes," said Jessie. "But don't forget, we have to shop for groceries and make the beds so we can sleep here tonight."

"I know," said Benny as he rushed across the room. The others followed him into a long dining room. A table with twelve chairs around it took up most of the room.

"Who are those portraits of?" asked Henry, pointing to the oil paintings of a man and a woman that hung above the long table.

"The Taylors," Grandfather said. "They are distant relatives of ours. In fact, they lived in the house before Aunt Sophie."

"Mrs. Taylor sure is pretty," said Violet. The young woman in the painting sat under a tree on a plaid blanket. She wore a long, white lace dress with a high collar. Her blond hair was tucked under a wide-brimmed straw hat.

"Yes, she was," Grandfather agreed. "She died young, not long after that portrait was painted."

"Oh, how sad," said Violet.

"Let's not think about that," said Henry. "There's a lot more to explore."

Indeed there was. The house had a ball-room, an enormous kitchen with a pantry, a library, and six bedrooms on the second floor.

"Why do all the bedrooms have fireplaces?" Benny wanted to know.

"This house was built in the days before central heating," answered Grandfather. "They needed fireplaces to heat the rooms."

Benny and Henry decided to share a big bedroom with a window seat. Jessie and Violet picked the one with the big four-poster bed in it. Grandfather chose the little bedroom he had slept in as a boy.

The Aldens were very busy. Henry and Benny unloaded the car and brought in all the bags. Jessie and Violet found sheets and towels in the big closet near the kitchen and began to make the beds.

When all the beds were made, Grandfather took his grandchildren out to eat at a local diner. "We can shop for groceries tomorrow," he told Jessie.

"Yes, I'm starving," said Benny as the Aldens all piled into the car. "You know, I didn't have much lunch."

Jessie laughed. "Yes, Benny. I know."

"Look how dark it is," said Violet as Grandfather started the car. She looked at her watch. "It's only six o'clock."

"It gets dark early here in the fall and winter," Grandfather explained. "We're farther north than in Greenfield, so the sun sets earlier."

"Oh," said Violet.

The moon was rising as Grandfather drove down Aunt Sophie's long, winding driveway. None of them noticed the blond girl in the tower window who was watching everything they did.

CHAPTER 3

A Nosy Waitress

Violet was the first one awake the next morning. She put on her fuzzy slippers and tiptoed out of the room she shared with Jessie. It was so quiet in the hallway, Violet could hear the floorboards creak. She walked toward the ballroom and stepped inside. As she looked around the large, airy room, she imagined couples from long ago dancing in the night.

"Boo!" someone shouted behind her. Violet jumped.

"I didn't mean to scare you." Benny was

laughing. He walked over to Violet in his fuzzy slippers. "Isn't this room huge?"

Violet nodded. "I wonder what it was like to live here when people used this room for dances," said Violet, looking up at the high chandeliers that each held twelve candles. Folding chairs and small tables were stacked in one corner of the room. In another were some old chairs covered with a sheet.

"Do you think Great-aunt Sophie gave balls in here?" asked Benny.

"Well, yes," answered Violet. "But this room does not seem as if it's been used in a while. Look how dusty everything is. We've got some work to do."

"Oh, Violet, Benny, there you are," said Jessie, who stood by the door. "Grandfather is taking us all out to breakfast."

"Oh, goody," said Benny.

Half an hour later, the Aldens were seated at a booth in the Jarvi Bakery in downtown Brockton.

"Boy, these pancakes are delicious," said

Benny as he poured more raspberry syrup over them.

"They're called pan-nu-kak-ku," said Grandfather. He pronounced each syllable slowly. "They're Finnish pancakes."

"They taste better than regular pancakes," said Henry. "They're like a combination of a pancake, an omelet, and custard."

Benny nodded. His mouth was full.

"I couldn't help overhearing how much you like the *pannukakku*," said the waitress when she came over to refill Grandfather's coffee. "You know, there is a Finnish special on the menu every day."

"Are all the specials as good as these pancakes?" asked Benny after he had swallowed his food.

"Oh, yes," answered the waitress, who was young and blond. "At least I think so. You're staying in the old Taylor mansion, aren't you?"

"How did you know that?" Benny looked very surprised.

"I saw you from my window," the waitress answered. "I rent an apartment on the third floor."

"For heaven's sake," said Grandfather. "So you're the other tenant. I am James Alden, and these are my grandchildren: Henry, Jessie, Violet, and Benny."

"Yes, I know," said the waitress, extending her hand to Grandfather. "I'm pleased to meet you. My name is Kimberly Watson. I just moved here a couple months ago from California. I used to talk to your aunt all the time. She was really nice."

"How do you know about us?" asked Benny.

"Your great-aunt Sophie told me all about her family in Greenfield. Even though she never met you, she felt she knew you through your grandfather's letters."

"Oh," said Benny, looking pleased.

"How do you like living in Brockton?" asked Grandfather.

Kimberly shrugged. "Well, it's really different up here. I'm not used to this cold weather, or . . ." Kimberly paused and twirled her long hair. Violet noticed she wore a ring on every finger, except her thumb.

"Or what?" Henry asked, when it seemed as though Kimberly was not going to finish her sentence.

"Uh, never mind," said Kimberly. "So, I hear you're selling the old house." She seemed eager to change the subject.

"Yes," answered Grandfather. "We'll be going through my aunt Sophie's papers and belongings. I plan to sell the house complete with the furniture. Unless there are any pieces my grandchildren want," he added, smiling at them.

"Well, let me know if you need any help," said Kimberly. "I know all about your aunt Sophie's things. We spent quite a bit of time together."

"Really?" said Grandfather.

"Oh, yes," said Kimberly importantly. She looked as if she wanted to keep talking to the Aldens, but more customers were coming into the bakery. She rushed off to take their orders.

*   *   *

On the way home, the Aldens stopped off at the grocery store, then the hardware store, where they bought brooms, mops, pails, rags, and other cleaning supplies.

"Brockton sure is pretty," said Violet as the Aldens walked to their car. Old sandstone buildings lined Brockton's Main Street. In the distance, the Aldens could see rolling hills covered with pine trees and Victorian-style houses.

"Wow, all these houses look about one hundred years old," said Benny.

"Some of them are," Grandfather answered. "Many of them were built at the same time as Aunt Sophie's."

When the Aldens returned to Aunt Sophie's house, they were very busy. First they unloaded the car and put away all their groceries and supplies. Then Grandfather went upstairs to his aunt Sophie's study to begin sorting out all her papers. Henry, Jessie, Violet, and Benny swept the ballroom and moved all the broken furniture to the woodpile outside.

"We can sell the pieces that are in pretty

good shape with the house," said Henry. "The rest we can use as firewood."

By lunchtime the ballroom sparkled. "It looks good enough to give a party in here," said Jessie proudly as she shook out her broom.

The others nodded. "I think we should eat after all this hard work," said Henry.

"Good idea," said Violet. Benny was already on his way to the kitchen.

"I'll make tuna salad for sandwiches," said Violet as she took out a big bowl and mixed together tuna, mayonnaise, lemon juice, salt, and pepper. Henry sliced some bread. Jessie and Benny set the table with Aunt Sophie's blue-and-white dishes. They also made lemonade, mixed a green salad, and put potato chips on every plate.

"My, this looks like a good lunch," said Grandfather when he came downstairs.

It began raining right after lunch.

"Oh, I wish it would snow," said Benny, sighing. "Now we can't even go outside."

"No, but there is a lot to explore inside

this house," Henry reminded his brother.

"That's true," said Benny, beaming as he remembered the old wooden rocking horse in the kitchen closet.

When the Aldens finished drying the dishes, Benny rushed over to the secret closet. Grandfather returned to sorting Aunt Sophie's papers. Violet decided to look in the library for something to read.

"That's a good idea," said Jessie, following her.

The library was lined with floor-to-ceiling bookshelves that held rows and rows of leather-bound books.

"We shouldn't have a problem finding something to read in here," said Jessie as she started reading the book titles on the shelf nearest to her. "Look, here are some fairy tales with gorgeous illustrations."

"Really?" said Violet. Her eyes shone. Violet loved to draw. "Oh, let me see."

Carefully, Jessie handed Violet a big book covered in red leather. Violet sat right down in one of the many armchairs in the library and began to look at it. Jessie kept exploring. She saw books written by Charles Dickens, Washington Irving, and Robert Louis Stevenson. She also found books about trees, wildflowers, and rocks and minerals. "Hmm," she said. "I wish I could find a good mystery."

Violet looked up from her book for just a moment. "There are more books on that shelf over there," she said, pointing.

Jessie went over to the dusty shelf. It seemed as though the oldest books in the library lay on it. There was a book of Irish poems and riddles and next to it a book of maps that was so old, the yellowed paper tore as soon as Jessie touched it.

"This was not what I had in mind," said Jessie as she put down the maps. That was when she noticed another book, a small book with a dark cover, wedged behind the others. Carefully she pulled the little book out and blew the dust off it. The title MY BOOK was engraved in gold letters across the cover. Inside, written in blue ink, were the words: *The Diary of Emily Rebecca Taylor, 1900.*

CHAPTER 4

The Diary

"Oh, Violet, come here. Look what I found!" cried Jessie.

"What?" Violet seemed very reluctant to leave her book, but looked up when Jessie came toward her.

"A diary." Jessie was already flipping through the pages. Though they were yellow with age, they did not fall apart when Jessie touched them. Violet bent over the book, as excited as Jessie. The handwriting belonged to a young girl who wrote in script. Some of the words were crossed out

or smudged from the fountain pen, which made the diary hard to read.

Brockton, Michigan
8 November 1900
This diary was a present from Father for my twelfth birthday. I am going to write in it every week.

"Oh, she's just my age," said Jessie. She could not believe that a girl who had sat in this library, perhaps in the very chair Violet had just been sitting in, was writing in her diary almost one hundred years ago.

Today, Father gave me a lovely tea party. All my dolls came, including Samantha, who is very old. I dressed her in a long pink dress with a lace collar.

Betsy and Ann, my best friends from school, came to the party, too. So did Mother, who felt well enough to come downstairs. That made the party extra special.

We ate cream cakes and gingerbread and drank real tea with lemon in it. Because it was my birthday, Mother gave us permission to use Grandmother's special blue-and-white china.

"I wonder if that's the china we used at lunchtime," said Jessie. "Emily can tell us so much about this house."

Violet nodded as she wrapped her arms around her shoulders. "I can't believe you found this. Let's show the others."

When Grandfather saw the diary, he held it in his hands and just stared at it. "You know, Emily is the daughter of the couple whose portraits are in the dining room."

"Oh, no, not of the woman who died," Violet said.

Grandfather nodded.

Soon all five Aldens were seated around the kitchen table listening while Jessie read the diary aloud.

17 November 1900
Mother is still very weak, so weak there are days she does not leave her bed. I visit her when I come home from school. We still laugh and

talk, but I can tell she is very tired. She has been teaching me to write sonnets and riddles. Mother loves poetry. Today we wrote a riddle together about a clock. Here it is:

I run around in circles, yet my path is always straight.
I can be quiet or noisy; sometimes I am late.

Of size and shape, I have many. I come in circles or squares.
And some, seeing me sit so calmly, think I have no cares.

If I run slower or faster, things do not work as smoothly.
So I try to be on time not to upset things unduly.

Can you guess what I am?

"Wow," said Benny. "I wouldn't be able to guess that was a clock."

"She does give us lots of clues, though," Jessie said. "Like here when she's talking about being late, running slower or faster, and being on time." Jessie pointed out the words to Benny as she talked.

Benny nodded. "Oh, now I understand."

Jessie continued reading:

24 November 1900

I can tell Father is very worried about Mother. He has been ever since she fell from her horse last month. The doctor now comes to the house to visit her almost every other day.

There wasn't another entry until December 15:

I have not been able to write in my diary in a long time. Mother died on December first.

"How sad," said Jessie.

"She was awfully young to lose her mother," said Grandfather. The children nodded.

21 December 1900

Mother left me her diamond engagement

*ring, and many other things like her linens and
lace. Father says the ring is very valuable, and
I should keep it in a safe place. It is a beautiful ring with a pearl and a diamond on a high
setting. Here is a picture of it:*

3 January 1901

I have put the ring in a little box with some
of Mother's lace handkerchiefs. I have hidden it
in a special place that meant a lot to Mother
and me, and I have not told anyone where it is,
not even Father.

"I wish she would tell her diary where it is," said Benny.

"Maybe she does," said Jessie as she turned the page.

"The ring may no longer be in the house," said Grandfather. "No doubt Emily took it with her when she grew up and moved away."

"Here is a long entry about a sleigh ride Emily took with Betsy and Ann," said Jessie.

"I want to hear more about the ring," said Benny.

"Oh, I found something," said Jessie. "Here Emily says she's practicing her riddle writing. And she's written a riddle about where the ring is hidden."

"Oh, Jessie, please read it!" Benny was so impatient, he wiggled in his chair.

Jessie cleared her throat. "A riddle by Emily Rebecca Taylor," she began:

My ring lies near the waiter who brings me up my tea.

As I hear his creaking sounds,
I hope my ring will not be found — by any-
one but me.

When Jessie finished, the others looked at one another. "What does she mean?" asked Benny. "It doesn't make any sense."

"We need to think about it," said Henry. "Maybe there are more clues in the diary." He bent over the little book while Jessie flipped the pages. There were more entries about Emily's mother, her family, her friends, her riding lessons, and her parties, but no other clue about the ring.

"Skip to the end," Benny suggested.

Jessie nodded. "Oh, here's something," she said.

19 September 1906
Tomorrow I will be leaving to go study in England. How I will miss Father and this house where I have so many memories of Mother! I

do hope Father will not be too lonely, but he travels so much with his work.

I am taking many of Mother's dresses with me to England. Most of her clothes fit me now, but I have decided not to take the ring. It is too valuable and I do not want to risk losing it overseas. I am leaving it in this house, where it will always be safe in its hiding place.

"Is that it?" asked Benny. "That's the last page?"

Jessie nodded and held out the book to show Benny.

"That's means the ring might still be here — right in this house. Maybe even in the library." Benny got up and looked around the room, wondering where there might be a good hiding place.

Jessie closed the diary. "Grandfather, do you know if Emily ever came back to this house?" she asked.

Grandfather did not answer right away. "I don't believe so," he finally said.

"That means the ring could very well still be in this house," said Jessie.

Benny hopped up and down. "I knew it. I knew it!" he exclaimed. "We should start looking right now."

The others laughed. "Benny, it's been here all these years. It's not likely to disappear overnight," Henry pointed out.

"Oh, Benny, look out the window," said Violet. "It's snowing."

CHAPTER 5

A Little Door

"It's snowing really hard," said Benny, beaming. He pressed his nose against the windowpane in the library. Already snow was piling on the ledge outside and on the tree branches. "It never snows in Greenfield this early in the year."

"No," agreed Grandfather. "Not usually."

"So, Benny, what are we waiting for?" said Henry. "Let's go outside and play."

"But what about the riddle?" said Benny. "We need to find the ring before we leave."

"We have time," said Violet. "Besides,

maybe we can think better when we're outside."

"You know," said Henry, "I saw lots of skis and snowshoes in the kitchen closet. Do you think we could try them?"

"Certainly," said Grandfather. "See if they're your size. By the time you're all ready, there may be enough snow on the ground for a practice run."

Grandfather followed his grandchildren as they raced toward the kitchen closet. Henry reached the closet first. He pulled open the door and started to take out ski poles, skis, even ski boots.

"There are enough for all of us, and they're all sorts of sizes." Henry sounded pleased. "Even small ones for Benny."

"Ah, some old cross-country skis," said Grandfather, smiling.

"How are they different from regular skis?" asked Violet.

"Cross-country skis allow you to glide even on flat ground. That way you can ski in the backyard, in the woods, almost anywhere there's snow," explained Grandfather.

"With the other kind of skis, you need mountains," added Henry.

"Right," said Grandfather. "And since there are no high mountains in Brockton, most people go cross-country skiing. It's a very popular sport around here. Most of the ski trails were laid out by the Finnish settlers."

"I can't wait to try," said Violet, who already had her shoes off. She reached for a pair of ski boots.

"What about ski wax?" asked Jessie. "We don't have any."

Grandfather had a twinkle in his eye. "I picked some up when we were grocery shopping," he said. "I thought we should be prepared."

"Oh, Grandfather, you think of everything," said Jessie admiringly.

By the time the Aldens were ready, it was snowing harder than ever. The wind whipped through the branches of the pine trees, blowing snow all over Henry, Jessie, Violet, and Benny as they skied through the backyard. The soft winter light made the snow sparkle.

"It's too bad Watch isn't here," said Jessie as she slid across the snow, then fell. She planted one of her ski poles firmly on the ground to push herself up. Soon Benny fell, too, then Henry. But not Violet. She glided across the snow, using her poles to help her.

"Violet, you're a natural," Henry said, looking very impressed.

Violet laughed. "It's sort of like walking, except you have to remember you're on skis."

Aunt Sophie's yard was enormous. Oak, pine, and maple trees surrounded the spacious lawn. Near the house were flower beds of all shapes and sizes. No plants were in bloom now, but their vines covered the ground like a thick gray mist.

Beyond the flower beds, the Aldens had plenty of room to practice turning, gliding, falling, and getting up again.

"Maybe we can go on one of the ski trails tomorrow," said Henry as he circled a pine tree. "I think I'm getting the idea now."

"Me, too," said Benny just as the tip of one of his skis hit a rock — and down he fell. "Maybe I shouldn't have said anything," he said, laughing.

After more practice, Benny felt confident enough to follow Henry, Jessie, and Violet into the woods behind the lawn.

There, the trees grew so thickly, their branches blocked out most of the sunlight. "Look, there's a little trail through the woods." Henry pointed it out with his ski pole.

"It's awfully dark in here," Benny said. He tried to keep up with the others, but his ski poles kept getting tangled in the brush.

"Benny, take your time," Henry called reassuringly. "We don't have to go too far into the woods."

"Oh, look, a chipmunk," Benny said. The chipmunk scurried in front of Benny, then hid in a clump of bushes growing on one side of the trail.

Before they decided to turn back, the Aldens saw three red squirrels, two deer, and a flock of geese circling overhead.

"I bet those geese are going south for the winter," observed Jessie.

"Probably," Henry agreed. "You know, some of these animals seem awfully tame," said Henry. "I'm surprised that chipmunk and those squirrels came so close to us."

"Maybe someone feeds them," said Jessie.

"Maybe," said Henry.

"You know, it's getting really cold out here, and I'm hungry," Benny hinted.

"It certainly is cold," agreed Jessie as she wrapped her wool scarf more tightly around her neck. "Come on, Benny, I'll race you home."

Jessie took the lead, and Benny followed. When he came near the flower beds, Benny kept his eyes on the ground in front of him so he could steer around the vines. That was why he did not see the man in the brown tweed coat until it was too late.

Benny and the man ran right into each other, and both fell in the snow.

"Oops," said Benny.

Professor Schmidt glared at Benny as he dusted snow off his wool trousers. He did not appear to be hurt. Neither was Benny, but he was so embarrassed he could feel his cheeks turn bright red.

"Would you please watch where you are going?" said the professor as he took off his spectacles and wiped the snow off with a handkerchief. "It's dangerous to race around in this weather. Besides, this garden is not a good place for skiing."

"I know," said Benny. "And I'm, uh, really sorry, sir. I didn't look where I was going."

"That's obvious," answered the professor as he continued on his way. Henry, Jessie, Violet, and Benny watched as the professor walked slowly across the lawn and into the woods.

"He doesn't seem very nice," said Benny when the professor was out of earshot.

Henry nodded. "We just need to stay out of his way," he said. "He made that clear the first time we met him."

"I wonder why he doesn't like children," said Jessie.

When the Aldens returned to the house,

they gathered in the kitchen. Jessie put a pan of milk on the stove to heat for hot chocolate. The others hung their damp jackets on the coatrack by the kitchen door.

Benny was the first one to notice another little door that did not reach all the way to the floor. He had to stand on tiptoe to open it. And when he did, he found himself staring into a dark opening. Inside was a wooden platform with two ropes on one side of it.

"It looks like an elevator shaft," said Jessie as she poked her head inside the little door. She could see that the platform had a roof and two sides. It looked like a box. When Jessie looked up, she could see a big wheel that turned when she pulled on one of the ropes.

"Oh, look, you just made the platform go higher," said Benny as he poked his head inside the opening, too.

"You know what this is, don't you?" asked Henry, looking very excited.

"What?" asked Benny.

"It's a dumbwaiter." Henry made sure to

say the word *waiter* very clearly. "It's used to send food from the kitchen up to the other floors," he explained.

"Why do they call it that?" asked Benny.

"It brings you food like a waiter, but it doesn't talk, so it's called dumb," answered Henry.

"But it makes some noise," Violet pointed out. "Look how much it creaked when you pulled on the rope."

"Exactly," said Henry, looking at the others. Just like the waiter in the riddle."

"Oh!" exclaimed Benny.

"Of course! Why didn't I think of that?" said Jessie. She pulled a piece of paper out of the pocket of her jeans. "Here's the riddle. I copied it down," she said.

My ring lies near the waiter who brings me up my tea.

As I hear his creaking sounds,

I hope my ring will not be found — by anyone but me.

Benny was so excited, he jumped up and down. "That's it. This has to be the waiter Emily wrote about."

Henry nodded. "Now all we have to do is look on every floor of the house, near the dumbwaiter."

"For the special place Emily talks about in her diary," added Violet.

Benny wanted to start looking for the ring right away. But the others convinced him to eat dinner first. Then the Aldens were so tired from their skiing and cleanup efforts, they went right to bed.

"I hope we find the ring tomorrow," Benny told Jessie as she tucked him in.

CHAPTER 6

Afternoon Tea

The next day, Henry, Jessie, Violet, and Benny began to look for the ring right after breakfast.

"We should probably look in the kitchen closet near the dumbwaiter," said Benny.

"I don't think we need to," said Jessie. "The riddle says, 'My ring lies near the waiter who brings me *up* my tea.'"

"Oh, that's true," said Benny, who was already on his way to the second floor. There, the Aldens found the dumbwaiter door and looked inside. Benny pulled on the rope.

The wooden platform creaked and rattled. Soon it was on the second floor.

"I'm going to ride in it," Benny announced.

"Go ahead. It's plenty strong, and you're the only one small enough to fit," said Henry as he held the platform steady while Benny scrambled onto it.

"Oh, boy," said Benny. "This is almost as fun as an amusement park."

"Do you see any openings in the wall, someplace where a little box could be hidden?" asked Henry.

"The riddle says the ring is *near* the dumbwaiter, not *in* it," Jessie reminded them.

"I know," said Henry. "But it's a good idea to check anyway."

"I don't see anything," said Benny as he felt the walls inside the dumbwaiter with his hands. "But it's very dark in here. I think I need a flashlight."

"I'll get you a flashlight," said Jessie. "There's one in the kitchen."

In no time at all, Jessie was back with the

flashlight, which she handed to Benny.

"Okay, hold on, I'll send you up to the next floor," Henry told Benny.

"I'm ready," said Benny as he made himself comfortable.

Henry pulled one of the ropes and Benny went higher and higher.

"Ah-choo! Ah-choo!"

"Benny?" called Henry as he looked up the dumbwaiter shaft. "Are you all right?"

"All this dust is getting in my nose," answered Benny. His voice sounded muffled.

"Are you at the next floor yet?" Henry called.

"How can I tell?" asked Benny.

"There should be a little door in the wall like this one," Henry explained.

"Oh," said Benny. "Yes, I see a bolt like the one on your floor."

"Do you see anything near the door?" asked Henry.

It took Benny a long time to answer. "No," he finally called.

"Can you go farther?" asked Henry.

"Yes," said Benny. Henry pulled on the

rope. Benny rode up to the attic. Then he had Henry bring him down to the kitchen. Then back up to the second floor.

"This is so much fun," said Benny as he climbed out of the dumbwaiter. He had dirt and dust in his hair and on his arms, hands, and face.

"Oh, Benny, you look like a chimney sweep," said Jessie, laughing.

"A what?" asked Benny.

"Someone who cleans chimneys," answered Jessie.

"There was a lot of dust up there," said Benny. Violet handed her little brother a packet of tissues from her pocket.

"Well, what are we waiting for?" asked Benny after he had blown his nose and wiped his face.

The Aldens searched and searched. On the second floor, near the dumbwaiter, they found closets full of clothes, sheets, and towels.

"Nothing here," said Benny as he walked out of the linen closet.

"Well, there's actually a lot in that

closet," said Henry. "Just no ring."

"Not even a box that could hold the ring," said Violet. "Remember, Emily said she put the ring in a box with other things from her mother."

Henry nodded.

"Don't forget, we have to be quiet on this floor," said Jessie as the Aldens walked up the staircase to the third floor. "We don't want to disturb the professor."

"I'll say," Benny whispered as he tiptoed up the rest of the stairs. At the top, he looked around, trying to guess which door belonged to the professor.

Henry found the dumbwaiter at the end of the hallway. "There isn't a closet on this floor," he said. "At least not one near the dumbwaiter."

"Good," said Benny. "I was getting tired of looking at sheets and towels."

Violet laughed. "If you were Emily, where would you hide a ring?"

"In a safe place," said Jessie. "Maybe even in a safe." Jessie laughed a little at her joke.

"A what?" asked Benny.

"A safe," Jessie repeated. "It's a place where people keep their most valuable things."

"Safes are usually built into the wall," said Violet as she took a painting of a trumpet off the wall so she could look behind it.

"We should look behind all these paintings and the furniture," said Henry as he moved a heavy armchair away from the wall.

The Aldens looked and looked. They found coins, bobby pins, and spools of thread, but no ring.

"I wish Emily had given us more clues," said Henry as he hung a big mirror back on the wall.

"Clues," said a loud voice. "What were you looking for behind that mirror?" Kimberly came bounding up the steps holding a leash with a miniature white poodle on the end.

"Is that your dog?" asked Henry, happy to change the subject.

Kimberly nodded. Her cheeks were flushed from the cold. She wore several scarves tied loosely around her neck, above her hot pink jacket.

"This is Juniper." Kimberly picked up her dog so Henry could pet it. "I take her out for a walk every day, but she really isn't used to snow."

Henry patted Juniper's curly white fur. Juniper whined and gave a shrill bark. "She's cute," he said.

"So what are you doing on this floor?" Kimberly asked. "And what is all this talk about clues?"

"Oh, nothing really," said Henry.

"You are looking for something, aren't you?" said Kimberly.

"Well, yes," Henry admitted. "But, uh, it's nothing important. We'd better go." The others nodded and hurried down the stairs before Kimberly could say anything more. The Aldens heard her close the door to her apartment with a loud bang. Even so, they waited a little while before they ventured up the stairs again to the attic.

The attic was a big room filled with trunks, old toys, hatboxes, and shelves that held books, blocks, tops, baseballs, and clocks.

"There is a lot to explore here," said Violet as she went over to look at a mannequin dressed in a long black cape.

"First let's find the dumbwaiter," said Henry. "It's a good thing you brought the flashlight." Although there was a bare lightbulb hanging from the ceiling, it did not produce much light.

Henry moved the flashlight along all the walls very carefully. "Maybe we can find an opening in one of the walls," he said. The Aldens looked and looked, but they did not see anything that looked like a door.

"Where is the dumbwaiter?" asked Benny. "I know I went up two floors from where I started."

Henry looked a little discouraged.

"I have a feeling the ring is in this attic," said Jessie as she sat down on the floor and leaned against a steamer trunk. "We've searched the other floors really carefully. It has to be up here."

"Maybe we should look inside some of these trunks," said Violet. She fiddled with a padlock.

"I don't know," said Henry. "Those trunks may not have belonged to Emily or her mother. Look, this one has Great-aunt Sophie's name on it." Henry held the flashlight above the trunk so Violet could read the leather name tag.

Violet nodded thoughtfully. "That's true. Emily probably would not hide the ring in a trunk or on a shelf, where the box would be in plain sight."

"I bet she hid the ring in a closet or, like you said, in a safe," Benny said as he looked around the big attic and up at the rafters. "Hey, wait a minute," he exclaimed. He had just noticed that the ceiling continued above a wall that did not reach all the way to the rafters. There's a room behind that wall!" Benny was so excited he was shouting.

"You're right," said Henry as he rushed over to the wall. Carefully he examined every square inch with his flashlight. "Aha, here's a keyhole." Henry shone his flashlight on the iron fitting.

"But we don't have a key," Violet pointed out.

"Wait," said Jessie. "I saw some keys hanging on the wall near the trunks." She rushed over to the other side of the attic.

"I saw those, too," said Benny, following her.

"Look, these keys are labeled," Jessie said to Benny. "Workshop, sewing room, library, hall closet, and attic!"

Jessie ran toward Violet and Henry with the attic key in her hand. She took a deep breath and fit the key into the lock.

"It fits! It fits!" cried Benny.

Jessie nodded. It took two hands to do it, but the lock finally did turn. The Aldens looked at one another.

"What do you think we'll find in there?" asked Benny excitedly.

Slowly, Jessie pushed the door open.

It took a while for their eyes to adjust to the dim light in the room, but when they

did, they could not believe what they saw.

Inside were six dolls seated around a table. They were having a tea party. On the table were blue-and-white china plates, a teapot, a sugar bowl, a pitcher, and cups and saucers. One doll held a small spoon in her hand. Another had her arms around her teacup.

A thick layer of dust covered everything in the room. Cobwebs hung from the ceiling. And the dim noonday light slanted through a little window that was covered with grime.

CHAPTER 7

A Discovery

Jessie was the first to find her voice. "Look, the dolls are using the blue-and-white china Emily mentioned in her diary."

"And this doll is probably Samantha," said Violet as she walked over to a dark-haired doll in a faded pink dress.

"You know," said Henry, "this could very well be the special place Emily talks about in her diary. The place that meant so much to her — and her mother."

The others nodded. "And besides," said

Benny, "they are all having tea. Emily talks about tea in the first line of her riddle."

"That's right," said Henry.

"Oh, I just know the ring is in this room," said Benny.

"Well, the obvious place to look is near the dumbwaiter," said Henry.

"Right," said Jessie as she looked around the room for a little door.

"Here's the dumbwaiter," said Benny as he rushed over to the far wall. He poked his head inside the dumbwaiter's door. He noticed a small hole near the dumbwaiter's shaft. "Oh, look," he said excitedly, "this would be a great place to hide the ring."

While the others looked over his shoulder, Benny put his fingers in the hole. Plaster crumbled from the wall.

"Did you find it?" asked Violet.

Benny shook his head. "No, there's nothing here."

The Aldens searched and searched. They looked inside and outside the dumbwaiter, in all the cracks in the wall, under tables and chairs and dishes, and in all the corners and crannies of the room.

They went downstairs for lunch and came back with their grandfather and more flashlights. Still they could not find the ring.

"Oh, where could it be?" Benny said.

"I don't know," said Henry, shaking his head. "We've looked everywhere in this room."

"Do you think someone found the ring before us and took it?" asked Jessie.

"It's possible," said Grandfather. "But it doesn't look like anyone has been in this room in a very long time."

"Not with all that dust on the dolls and furniture," Violet agreed.

"I don't remember ever seeing this room before," said Grandfather. "Not in all the summers I visited." He shook his head. "You children are discovering all kinds of things in the old mansion," he added proudly.

"But not the ring," said Henry.

Jessie brushed her long brown hair away from her face with her wrist. "I guess we may not find it after all," she said.

"Then Emily will get her wish," said Benny.

"What do you mean?" asked Violet.

"She says in the riddle she hopes no one ever finds the ring but her," said Benny.

Jessie rumpled Benny's hair. "You're right," she said, laughing.

In the next few days, the Aldens tried to forget all about the ring. They cleaned out closets, packed books, dusted furniture, and mopped floors.

When they could, they went outside to enjoy the snow. They practiced their skiing, went sleigh riding, and took long walks in the woods.

"I love Brockton," said Violet as she walked in a snow-covered meadow with Jessie. Together the girls pulled a sled carrying Benny.

"Let's go around this big pine tree," called Benny. "Then I'll pull you."

"You'll pull both of us?" teased Jessie.

"Well, I don't know about that," said Benny, laughing.

"It's just so pretty here," said Violet. "We need to find a camera so we can take pictures of this place — and of the house. I wish Grandfather didn't have to sell it."

"I know. I'm sorry, too," said Jessie. "I agree. We should at least take pictures of it before we leave."

"I'm surprised we haven't found a camera in the house," said Violet as she tugged the sled over a mound of snow. "We've certainly found almost everything else."

"That's for sure," said Jessie, laughing.

That afternoon, Violet, Jessie, Henry, and Benny walked along Brockton's Main Street shopping for a camera.

"Could we get something to eat?" asked Benny as the Aldens walked past a small family-owned grocery store. Benny peered in the window. Inside were large tubs of freshly made ice cream.

"There's one flavor called Mackinac Island Fudge. And there's also vanilla and strawberry," said Benny hopefully.

"Benny, isn't it a little cold for ice cream?" asked Jessie.

"It's never too cold — or warm — for ice cream," Benny insisted.

"All right," said Jessie.

Mackinac Island Fudge turned out to be vanilla ice cream with big chunks of chocolate fudge in it. "Yum!" exclaimed Benny after he tasted a sample.

"It's named after Mackinac Island," said the grocery clerk. "An island in Lake Michigan about two hundred miles from here."

"That's far away," said Benny.

The clerk nodded and handed Benny a cone piled with two big scoops of ice cream. "No ice cream for the rest of you?" the clerk asked.

Violet shook her head. "No, thank you," she said.

Jessie scanned the stocked shelves in the store. "You know," she said, "I have an idea."

"What?" asked Benny. Vanilla ice cream dripped down his chin.

"We should give a little tea party," said Jessie. She pointed to the shelf loaded with tea, coffee, and cocoa.

"What a wonderful idea," said Henry.

Half an hour later, the Aldens emerged from the store. Jessie carried a shopping bag filled with bread, jam, cream, cocoa, and other goodies.

"When should we give our tea party?" asked Benny.

"Whenever we're in the right mood," answered Jessie. "But first let's find a camera."

The Aldens passed a sporting goods store, a bakery, an antique shop, and a deli. At the end of the block stood a small store with a big window displaying an antique desk, some oil paintings, an old radio, and a camera.

"Look," said Violet, pointing excitedly at the camera. "Let's go inside."

"Sam's Pawnshop," said Henry, reading the sign over the door.

"What's a pawnshop?" asked Benny as he

held the door open for the others.

"It's a store where you can sell your valuables," answered Henry. "If you need money, you can take your jewelry or whatever to a pawnshop, and they will buy it from you and sell it at a profit."

"But if you want to buy your things back, you can," added Jessie. "Provided the store hasn't already sold them."

"Oh," said Benny, looking down all the aisles. "This store sells everything." Indeed, the store was crammed with rocking chairs, old desks, books, paintings, posters, and toys. Display cabinets holding china dishes, vases, glasses, watches, and jewelry stood in the center of the store.

Violet asked to see the camera in the window. Henry walked to the back of the store to look at old comic books. Benny rushed over to the toys, and Jessie strolled around the big glass display cabinet looking at all the jewelry.

"Aren't those bracelets pretty?" asked the plump woman behind the counter. "Would you like to try one on?"

Jessie shook her head and walked on. Suddenly she stopped short and gasped. There, on a blue velvet cushion, lay a diamond and pearl ring — the same ring Emily had drawn a picture of in her diary!

CHAPTER 8

A Man Named Adam

"Are you all right?" asked the clerk anxiously, for Jessie looked like she had seen a ghost.

Jessie nodded and took a deep breath before she spoke. "Where did you get that ring?" she asked.

"Oh, that. Isn't it a beauty?" said the clerk. "I'm not sure. Sam, do you know who sold us the diamond and pearl ring?" she called loudly to the man helping Violet.

Sam walked over to the display case with Violet.

"Ring — did someone say something about a ring?" asked Benny as he, too, rushed over to the display case with Henry at his heels.

"Look," said Jessie, pointing.

Violet, Henry, and Benny gazed at the ring, their eyes wide. "Oh, you found it," Benny exclaimed. "Who brought it here?"

Sam scratched his head. "That's what I'm trying to remember," he said. Suddenly his eyes lit up. "Of course, Adam came in with it about two weeks ago."

"Adam?" asked Benny.

"Adam Tormala, I believe his name is. He's a big man. Wears glasses and a brown tweed overcoat."

"Does he live around here? May we speak to him?" asked Henry. "You see," he continued when he saw Sam's questioning look, "that ring belongs to our family."

"What?" Sam seemed more surprised than ever.

"It's a long story," said Jessie.

"I have time," Sam insisted. The clerk, who was called Judy, nodded also and arched her eyebrows. The Aldens could tell she did not want to miss a word.

Henry, Jessie, Violet, and Benny took turns telling Sam and Judy all about Great-aunt Sophie, Emily's diary, and their search for the ring.

When they finished, Judy shook her head. "That's unbelievable. I wonder where Adam got that ring."

"I don't know," said Sam. "But I'll give you children his address, and you can go ask him. I don't usually give out that information about my customers, but this is a special case."

"Thank you," said Jessie.

Sam pulled a blue pen out of his shirt pocket and scribbled on the notepad in front of him. "The man's name is Adam Tormala. That's a Finnish name."

"Everything seems Finnish around here," said Benny, remembering his delicious breakfast at the Jarvi Bakery.

"Well, yes, much of the Upper Peninsula was settled by people from Finland. They came to work in the copper mines," explained Sam.

"What about Mr. Taylor, the man whose portrait is on the wall of the dining room at Great-aunt Sophie's house? Was he from Finland?" asked Henry.

"Old Mr. Taylor. No, he was from England. He was one of the chief engineers in the mine where my ancestors worked," said Sam.

"Really," said Henry.

"Oh, yes," said Sam as he finished writing and pushed the pad across the counter to Henry. "In a small town like this, everyone knows about one another. Now, to find Adam's house, you can walk down Main Street and turn left at the light. Head up the hill three blocks and you'll see Jasper Lane on your right. His address is 42 Jasper Lane."

"Can we go right now?" asked Benny.

Jessie looked at her bag of groceries. "I don't see why not," she said. "These groceries will keep."

"Before we go, I'd like to buy that camera," said Violet.

Henry laughed. "I almost forgot about the camera," he said. "Does it work?"

"Yes, I checked to make sure when I bought it," Sam said.

The Aldens bought the camera. Then they wasted no time walking to Adam's house. On the way they passed several old Victorian-style houses, but none as grand as Great-aunt Sophie's.

Just before the Aldens turned onto Jasper Lane, they saw Professor Schmidt deep in conversation with a brunette woman. The woman held the leash of a beautiful dog with long golden fur.

Benny gulped when he saw the professor. Henry nodded at Professor Schmidt and said hello.

The professor nodded curtly and grunted something that sounded like "Good day." He did not look happy to see the Aldens.

"What a pretty dog," exclaimed Jessie as she stopped to pet the dog's soft fur.

"Thank you. Her name is Katie," the woman said.

The professor cleared his throat loudly. "You children are interrupting us. I was discussing Sarah's research project with her."

"Oh, sorry," Jessie said, looking flustered.

"Uh, we were just leaving," Henry muttered.

"Why is he always so rude to us?" asked Benny as the Aldens hurried down Jasper Lane.

"I guess he doesn't like to be interrupted when he's talking to a student," said Jessie.

"Let's not think about him," said Violet. She stopped in the middle of the street and pointed to a run-down house with yellow shutters. "This is number 42."

"This house is not in very good shape," Benny whispered as he climbed the sagging porch steps.

"No, it's not," agreed Jessie. The paint was peeling. The shutters hung crookedly from their hinges. The doorbell wasn't working.

"Knock loudly," Jessie suggested to Henry.

A tall, thin man with long red hair answered the door. He looked like he was in his early thirties.

"Could we speak to Adam Tormala, please?" asked Henry.

"You're speaking to him," the man said gruffly.

"Really? You're Adam Tormala?" Henry asked. Adam did not look at all the way Sam had described him.

"Isn't that what I just said?" Adam shivered a little in the cold, but he did not invite the Aldens inside. "What do you need to speak to me about?"

"You sold a ring that belongs to our family," Benny blurted out.

"What?" Now it was Adam's turn to look surprised. "What are you accusing me of?"

"You see," Henry began, "we're relatives of Sophie Taylor, and we're staying in her house right now."

The man nodded. "Yes, I heard you people were going to sell that old place. I knew

Sophie Taylor." He seemed a little less gruff now that he knew who the Aldens were.

"Would you like to come inside? I'm getting cold talking to you in the doorway." Adam held the door open wider.

The Aldens followed Adam through a small entryway and into the living room. Everywhere they looked, books and files were stacked against the wall. Adam did not own much furniture. The only two chairs in the living room looked like they would fall apart if anyone sat on them. Henry and Jessie sat on the lumpy couch. Violet and Benny sat on the wooden floor.

They told Adam about finding Emily's diary, about the clues she had left, and about the ring — the very same ring they had just seen in the pawnshop.

"I'm telling you, I don't know anything about your ring," Adam said.

"Were you in Sam's Pawnshop recently?" asked Henry.

"Well, yes, but I was in there pawning some of my furniture. You see, I'm trying to raise enough money to pay next semester's tuition. I hope to graduate this spring with my degree in history," Adam said.

"History," said Violet. "Do you know Professor Schmidt?"

Adam nodded. "Yes, I know him. He's my adviser. I sometimes do research for him."

"He's one of the tenants in our house," Benny said.

"I know," said Adam. "I've been up there to deliver some of my papers to him."

"Oh, so you've been in the house," said Henry.

Adam leaned forward and frowned. "Yes, I've been in the Taylor mansion. Most people in Brockton have, especially the ones who are interested in local history. That doesn't mean anything. How do you know the ring in the pawnshop is really Emily's?" Adam asked.

"There's a picture of it in the diary. The ring in the pawnshop looks *exactly* like it," Henry answered.

"Well," said Adam, "I was not the one who pawned it. Maybe you children should check your facts better. Sam has written records of whatever he buys."

"I'm pretty sure he was checking his records when he gave us your address," said Henry.

"Well, then his records are wrong," Adam said, frustrated. "If you want to file a charge against me, the police station is two blocks down on Main Street."

Henry held his breath for a moment. "We were hoping to clear this up without bothering the police."

"Well, you may *have* to bother them," said Adam as he got up. "Because I'm not going to stand for any more of this questioning. Leave my house, at once." He pointed to the door.

The Aldens looked at one another, then got up and hurried out of the room without saying another word.

"And don't you children ever bother me again, you hear?" Adam called after them, just before he slammed the door.

CHAPTER 9

The Evidence

"I hope we never have to talk to Adam again," said Benny as the Aldens hurried home. "He sure was unfriendly."

"I'll say," said Henry. The Aldens could see their footprints as the snow crunched underneath their boots. Snow was starting to pile up on the sidewalk.

"Adam might be telling the truth," said Violet as she pulled her purple scarf over her head.

Henry thought a moment before he answered. "He could be, but I have a feeling he's hiding something."

"Yeah," agreed Benny. "Why would he get so mad if he hasn't done anything?"

"One possibility," said Jessie, "is that Adam found the ring in the house when he was visiting the professor. We know he needs money. He probably couldn't resist selling it. And now he feels guilty."

"That may be why he got so angry whenever we mentioned the ring," added Henry.

"But," Violet said, "Adam did look very different from the person Sam described."

"That's true," Henry was forced to agree. "Maybe we should go back to the pawnshop and ask Sam some more questions."

Jessie looked at her watch. "It's four forty-five. If we hurry, we should have time to talk to Sam before the store closes."

Pink clouds dotted the sky as the Aldens rushed down Main Street. Sam was locking up the cash register as the Aldens walked in. "I'm locking up for the night," he informed them.

"We just need to ask you a couple more

questions," said Henry. He sounded a little out of breath from running.

"Ask away," said Sam. "Did you find Adam?"

Henry nodded. "We found him, but he wasn't too helpful."

"Really?" Sam shook his head. "Sorry to hear that."

"He said he never sold you that ring," said Violet.

Sam frowned. "I'm pretty sure he did."

"Do you have records we could check?" asked Violet. "That way, we could be sure."

Sam sighed. "I do keep records, but they're not up-to-date."

"Could we see them anyway?" Jessie persisted.

"Well, I don't know how I feel about that," said Sam. "You see, these records are confidential."

"Oh, I understand," said Jessie, but she looked very disappointed. They all did.

"I'll tell you what," said Sam as he shuffled papers around the counter. "Give me a couple of days, then come back. I should have the information you need."

"Thank you," said Jessie and Violet together.

"Do you think Sam knows more about this ring than he's letting on?" asked Jessie as the Aldens walked down Main Street.

"I don't know," said Benny as he broke an icicle off a low tree branch. "He's been so nice to us."

"Yes, he has, but he didn't give us the right description for Adam. And he wouldn't let us see his records," Jessie pointed out. The sun had just set over the hills, and a full moon was rising.

"Oh, Benny. Don't eat that icicle," said Jessie, taking her eyes off the moon long enough to look at her brother.

"Why not?" asked Benny. "It's clean water."

Jessie laughed. "Speaking of water," she said, "maybe we should walk home along the riverfront."

"Good idea," said Benny. "We haven't done that yet."

The Aldens turned and walked two

blocks down the hill from Main Street. Soon they were strolling on the dock alongside the waterway. Stars shone. Geese circled overhead, and the snow glistened in the moonlight.

The Aldens had not been walking long when they saw a girl sitting on a bench near the dock with her head in her hands. As they walked closer, they could see the girl was sobbing. She wore a hot pink ski jacket, a bright turquoise scarf, and pink earmuffs in her blond hair.

Benny poked Violet in the arm. "I think that's Kimberly," he whispered.

Violet nodded. "Should we ask her if she's all right?" she asked.

Jessie, Henry, and Benny looked like they didn't know what to do. Jessie started to approach the girl when suddenly she looked up. It was indeed Kimberly, and tears streamed down her face.

"I didn't know anyone was here," said Kimberly, sniffling. She took a pink tissue out of her pocket and blew her nose loudly.

"Are you all right?" asked Violet gently.

"Is there something we can do for you?" Jessie wanted to know.

Kimberly shook her head. "There's nothing anyone can do. I really must be going." Before the Aldens could say another word, Kimberly grabbed her black leather shoulder bag and quickly walked away.

Henry, Jessie, Violet, and Benny looked at one another. "I wonder what that was all about," said Jessie. "She's usually so anxious to talk to us. This time, she couldn't wait to get away."

"She was probably embarrassed we saw her crying," said Violet.

Jessie nodded. "Now, I wonder if maybe she's the one who found the ring and pawned it."

Violet's eyes widened. "You know, she could be. She was very interested in what we were looking for the other day."

"That's true," Henry agreed. "But as long as we're naming suspects, we should not forget about the professor."

"Professor Schmidt?" Jessie sounded surprised.

"Yes, why not?" said Henry. "He's made it clear he never wants to see us on his floor."

"He never wants to see us anywhere," Benny pointed out.

"Exactly," said Henry.

"Well, maybe," said Jessie. "But I still think Adam and Kimberly are our most likely suspects."

"I would not eliminate the professor or Sam," said Henry as he turned away from the dock and headed up the hill again.

"How are we going to find out who it is?" asked Benny. He had to run to keep up with Henry.

"We'll have to visit the pawnshop again in a couple of days," Henry answered. "In the meantime, we should keep a close eye on Professor Schmidt, Kimberly, Adam, and Sam."

"I'm glad it stays so cold here. None of our groceries spoiled," Jessie remarked as she rang the doorbell and waited for Grandfather to let them inside.

"Can we have our tea party tomorrow?" Benny asked.

Jessie nodded.

The next afternoon, Henry, Jessie, Violet, and Benny were very busy in the kitchen. "We should plan to have everything ready for four o'clock," Jessie reminded them. "That's the proper time for afternoon tea."

"We'll be ready," said Violet as she mixed flour, baking soda, and ginger together for gingerbread cookies. Henry was cutting a loaf of bread for cinnamon toast, and Benny and Jessie were making hot cocoa for themselves and tea for Grandfather.

"Don't you think we should invite Kimberly and the professor for tea?" Violet was teasing, but the others took her seriously.

"That might be a way to keep an eye on them," said Henry.

"And perhaps getting one of them to confess," said Jessie as she began to whip the cream.

"I don't think the professor is home right

now," said Benny. "I saw him head out toward the woods."

"And who knows what Kimberly is up to," said Henry as he began to set the dining room table.

An hour later, the Aldens called their grandfather downstairs for tea.

"Goodness, we haven't eaten in the dining room the whole time we've been here," said Grandfather as he sat down. Henry had set the table with Emily's blue-and-white china. Silver platters piled high with gingerbread, cinnamon toast, and tiny sandwiches lay on the table along with a big pot of tea and another of hot cocoa. There were also little pots of jam, sugar, and whipped cream.

"Please pass the cream and sugar," said Benny as he stirred his cocoa with a little spoon.

"This is so much fun," said Violet as she spread strawberry jam on her cinnamon toast. "No wonder Emily was always giving tea parties."

"If only she had left us with more clues," said Henry as he passed the sugar to Grandfather.

Benny nodded. "Well, she did leave us with that riddle. And she gave us the idea for this party." He bit into a gingerbread cookie. Suddenly his eyes opened wider, and he waved his arms wildly.

"Benny, what's wrong?" Jessie sounded truly alarmed. "Is something wrong with the gingerbread?"

Benny shook his head. "No, the gingerbread is fine," he answered, once he swallowed. "It's just that I thought of something important."

"What?" Jessie held her toast in midair. Everyone stopped eating and looked at Benny.

"The man Sam described — you know, the man who pawned the ring . . ."

"Yes," said Jessie.

"Well, Sam described the professor, not Adam." Benny sounded very proud of himself.

"You're right," said Henry. "He said he

was a big man with glasses. And he wore a brown tweed overcoat."

"Just like the professor," said Benny.

"It's true," said Violet. "The professor has worn a brown tweed overcoat every time we've seen him."

"It looks like we're going to have to ask Professor Schmidt a few questions," said Henry.

"I was hoping I wouldn't have to see him again," said Benny as he helped himself to another gingerbread cookie.

CHAPTER 10

The Professor

Soon everyone was talking at once. Henry wanted to go find the professor right away. The others convinced him to wait until they had talked to Sam. "That way, if Sam's records back us up, we'll have definite proof against the professor," said Jessie.

"But Sam said to give him a couple of days." Benny sounded disappointed. "That means we'll have to wait until tomorrow."

"Right," said Henry as he added whipped cream to his steaming mug of cocoa. "So we might as well sit here and enjoy our party."

"Well said," said Grandfather, reaching for a slice of cinnamon toast.

Violet looked up at the portraits of Emily's parents. Then she looked at her grandfather. He definitely looked a little like Emily's father.

"Grandfather?" Violet asked.

Grandfather looked up from pouring his tea. "Yes?"

Violet took a deep breath. What she wanted to say wasn't easy for her. "Grandfather," she began again, "do we really have to sell this house? I mean, it has so much family history in it."

Grandfather looked sad. "I know," he said. "It's a shame to let this house go out of the family. But we live too far away to be able to care for it properly."

"Could we try to find someone to take care of it for us?" asked Jessie hopefully. "We might be able to visit now and then. This would be a great place to take family vacations."

"I'll say," said Henry.

Grandfather gazed at his grandchildren, then up at the portraits. Emily's mother had the same hair, the same dreamy blue eyes as Violet. "We'll see," he said thoughtfully.

The next morning, Henry, Jessie, Violet, and Benny woke up early. They were at the pawnshop as soon as it opened.

"Well, you folks are certainly on the case," said Sam, who looked a little sleepy. "I just opened the store a few minutes ago."

"Were you able to check your records?" asked Jessie.

"Yes, yes," said Sam. "Now, let me see, what have I done with that note to myself?"

Jessie and Violet exchanged looks. They were no longer surprised Sam had been mixed up about the person who sold him the ring.

"Aha, here it is." Sam waved a paper in the air. "The person who sold me the ring is named Professor Francis Schmidt."

"I knew it! I knew it!" shouted Benny.

"Oh, dear. I guess I did lead you astray

when I said Adam had pawned the ring," said Sam, sighing. "No wonder he was upset. No one likes to be falsely accused."

"I guess not," said Violet, who suddenly felt very bad for Adam. "We should tell him we're sorry."

The others nodded. "But first let's find the professor," said Henry.

The Aldens met Professor Schmidt as he was walking across the lawn to the woods. "We have to talk to you," said Henry.

The professor looked at his watch. "What about?" he asked. "You see, this is usually the time I go feed the animals in the woods. They seem to expect me."

Benny stared at the professor. Never in his wildest dreams had he thought the professor cared about small animals. "What kind of food do you give them?" he asked.

"Mostly bread crumbs like this," answered the professor as he pulled some muffins out of his large pocket. "Now, what did you want to speak to me about?" he asked Henry.

"About a ring that belongs to our family," Henry replied.

"I did find a ring on the top floor of the house," said the professor. "It was in a hole in the wall."

"Was it a diamond and pearl ring with a silver band?" asked Jessie.

"A platinum band, I believe," answered the professor, looking surprised. "But yes, that describes it."

"And you took it and pawned it," Henry said.

The professor glared at Henry. "I did not *take* it, young man. I found it and told your great-aunt. But she insisted that I keep the ring."

"What?" Benny exclaimed.

"Did you show her the ring?" asked Violet more softly.

"Well, no," the professor admitted. "But I described it to her. She was quite ill then. You see, I found the ring a couple of months ago when I went upstairs to examine the roof. It was leaking. I was able to fix it, and your great-aunt was so grateful, she gave me the ring."

"Oh," said Henry and Jessie together.

"But why did you pawn it?" asked Benny.

The professor sighed. "Well, if you must know, I needed the money to send to my sister," he explained. "She's been ill."

The Aldens understood. They were beginning to understand the professor.

"Now, suppose you tell me what you know about the ring," said Professor Schmidt.

"It may take a long time," said Henry as he stamped his feet to keep them warm.

"Perhaps we had better go inside," the professor suggested.

Several minutes later, the professor sat in the living room with Henry, Jessie, Violet, Benny, and Grandfather. Jessie held Emily's diary on her lap. "Here is the part where Emily wrote about the ring," she said as she handed the book to the professor.

The professor looked at the drawing

carefully. Then he flipped the pages of Emily's diary and read the passages the Aldens pointed out. "This is fascinating," he said. "You've found a wonderful piece of local history here."

Grandfather gazed fondly at his four grandchildren. "They always manage to find important things, wherever they go," he said.

"You know, if I had known what this ring meant to your family and you, I never would have pawned it. In fact, let me go buy it back right away." The professor suddenly seemed in a great hurry. He grabbed his coat off the couch and rushed to the door.

"Why the rush?" asked Benny.

"He wants to get to the store before anyone buys the ring," Jessie explained.

"Oh, right," said Benny. "But we didn't get to ask him where he found the ring. It didn't sound like he was in the secret room."

"Don't worry, Benny. He'll be back," Grandfather assured him.

"Good. I want to tell him how we solved the riddle," said Benny.

Sure enough, the professor was back in twenty minutes, with Adam. He carried a blue velvet box in his hands.

"Adam Tormala, I'd like you to meet James Alden," said the professor. "Adam is one of my students. I hear he's met your grandchildren already." The professor's eyes twinkled.

Adam shook Grandfather's hand, but he barely glanced at Henry, Jessie, Violet, and Benny.

"I am very sorry about the misunderstanding with the ring," said Jessie.

"We all are," said Henry.

Adam looked solemn. "I accept your apology," he said. "Sam told me all about the mix-up when I talked to him this morning. I have no hard feelings, but I still think you children should check your facts more carefully before you go around accusing people."

"We will from now on," said Jessie.

"Yes," agreed the others, and they meant it.

"Adam is very interested in local history," the professor informed them. "I told him all about the discovery you children made. He'd like to see the diary and anything else you found."

"Sure," said Henry. "We didn't even get a chance to tell you about the secret room in the attic."

"And how we solved the riddle," added Benny.

"I want to hear all about it," said Adam eagerly.

"I do, too," said the professor. "But first let me give you the ring." The professor handed the little box to Grandfather.

Grandfather opened the box with trembling hands. "My, it's beautiful," he said as he held the ring up for everyone to see.

The professor fished in his deep pockets. "These are the lace handkerchiefs that were in the ring box. They belong to you, too."

"No one sews like that anymore," said Violet, admiring the fine lace. Although the handkerchiefs were yellow with age, they still looked good to the Aldens.

"And now let's go up to the attic," said Benny. On the way up the stairs, the Aldens told the professor and Adam all about finding the dumbwaiter, the doll's tea party, and the riddle.

"We knew the ring had to be in this little room," said Henry as he swung open the door.

"Goodness," exclaimed the professor as he looked at the dolls seated around the table.

"After we searched the room, we tried to put everything back just the way it was," said Jessie.

"Just the way Emily would have wanted it," added Violet. Her mind was faraway, in another era.

"And here is the dumbwaiter." Benny opened the little door.

"I see," said the professor, looking inside. "And you see, here, where the plaster is crumbling." The professor pointed to a small hole in the wall near the dumbwaiter's shaft.

"Yes, we looked in there," said Benny.

"Well, that's where Emily hid the ring. That hole goes through to the hallway. I found the box on the other side of this wall."

"I thought that would be a good hiding place for the ring," said Benny.

"You know," said Adam as he stooped down to examine the hole, "I bet Emily made this hole herself."

"That's what I was thinking," said the professor. "She could have made it with her father's geology pick. Then I think she tried to plaster it. See how the plaster looks different around the hole?"

The Aldens nodded. "Now that you mention it, it does," said Henry.

The Aldens followed the professor into the hallway. "Here's the hole where I found the ring," he said, pointing.

"It does go through to the attic room," said Benny as he bent down to examine the hole more closely.

"I don't think Emily wanted it to, though.

She probably wasn't used to making holes in the wall," said Henry.

"No, I'm sure she wasn't allowed to," Jessie agreed.

Adam and the professor stayed in the attic to look at all the old clothes, toys, and pictures. Then Grandfather suggested they come downstairs to his aunt's study so they could see her old letters.

"Don't you want to come, too?" he asked his grandchildren.

The Aldens looked at one another. They were now all on Kimberly's floor. "We'll come," said Jessie. "But there's something we'd like to do first."

As the others continued downstairs, Violet timidly knocked on Kimberly's door.

"Yes," Kimberly said when she opened the door.

"We just wanted to see how you were doing," said Violet.

"Oh," said Kimberly, looking a little embarrassed. "Please come in."

The Aldens sat in Kimberly's small living

room. Kimberly held Juniper on her lap and told the children how lonely she was up in Michigan. "I miss all my friends and family so much. I should never have come here to go to school. I don't like the climate; neither does my dog. And I haven't been able to make any friends, except for your great-aunt," she added.

The Aldens nodded. "Is that why you were crying last night?" asked Benny.

Kimberly nodded. "Sometimes I get so lonely I can't stand it. The people are so reserved up here."

"What?" asked Benny.

Kimberly smiled. "I mean they don't open up much to strangers, not like in California." Kimberly sighed. "But you know, I feel better now that I've decided to transfer to a school closer to home. I'll be leaving at the end of this term."

The Aldens stayed and talked to Kimberly for a long time. They invited her to go skiing and sleigh riding with them before they left.

"I'd love to," said Kimberly as she closed the door after them.

Henry, Jessie, Violet, and Benny found Grandfather in the living room with the professor and Adam. They were all laughing and talking.

"It sounds like a party down here," said Benny.

"In a way, it is," said Grandfather. "I have a surprise for you children."

"What?" they asked eagerly as they curled up by the fire near their grandfather.

"Well," Grandfather began, "I have decided not to sell this old house."

"Yippee!" shouted Benny. Jessie and Violet jumped up and hugged Grandfather. Henry beamed.

"Professor Schmidt has very kindly agreed to look after this house for us. He's quite handy at fixing things, and what's more, he really wants to do it," Grandfather said.

"I certainly do," said the professor. "I've always loved living in this old house. And

your grandfather has very generously agreed to let me live here for free. What's more, I'll have access to your aunt's papers and wonderful library for my research."

"That's wonderful," said Violet.

"I'm very pleased you're keeping this old place, Mr. Alden," Adam said. "It would be a shame to sell something with so much of your family's history in it."

"I agree," said Henry, smiling. Adam looked at him and winked.

"We should celebrate," said Violet.

"I know," said Jessie. "Let's have another tea party."

Everyone laughed.

GERTRUDE CHANDLER WARNER discovered when she was teaching that many readers who like an exciting story could find no books that were both easy and fun to read. She decided to try to meet this need, and her first book, *The Boxcar Children*, quickly proved she had succeeded.

Miss Warner drew on her own experiences to write the mystery. As a child she spent hours watching trains go by on the tracks opposite her family home. She often dreamed about what it would be like to set up housekeeping in a caboose or freight car — the situation the Alden children find themselves in.

When Miss Warner received requests for more adventures involving Henry, Jessie, Violet, and Benny Alden, she began additional stories. In each, she chose a special setting and introduced unusual or eccentric characters who liked the unpredictable.

While the mystery element is central to each of Miss Warner's books, she never thought of them as strictly juvenile mysteries. She liked to stress the Aldens' independence and resourcefulness and their solid New England devotion to using up and making do. The Aldens go about most of their adventures with as little adult supervision as possible — something else that delights young readers.

Miss Warner lived in Putnam, Connecticut, until her death in 1979. During her lifetime, she received hundreds of letters from girls and boys telling her how much they liked her books.

Puzzle It Out

It snows a lot in the Upper Peninsula of Michigan. In fact, it snows more there than anywhere else in the continental United States.

Henry, Jessie, Violet, and Benny love the snow. They know that once it stops falling, they can go skiing and skating, build snowmen, and even have a few snowball fights. But while a blizzard is raging, they have to stay inside.

But that's okay, too, because they can spend lots of time solving puzzles.

Are you stuck inside because of a storm? Never fear, the Boxcar Children Super Special puzzles are here! In fact, they start on the very next page!

You can check the answers to all of the puzzles on pages 132–135.

It's a Mystery!

It's wintertime! The snow is falling really hard, and the temperature is way below freezing. All you really want is a cup of hot cocoa, a yummy muffin, and a few good laughs.

If you're looking for something to do while you're stuck in the house, follow the maze below. After you find the right path, write down each of the letters as you come to them.

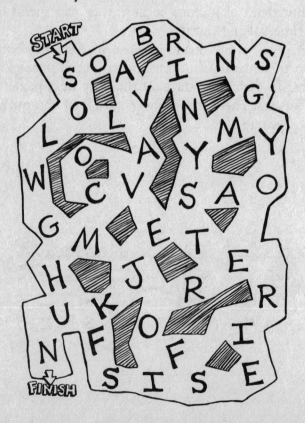

Outdoor Fun!

Hooray! The snow has stopped. Now the Aldens can go outside and play! But they don't know which cold-weather sport to try first. There are so many to choose from.

There are plenty of cold-weather sports hidden in this word search. The words go up, down, sideways, backwards, and diagonally. Look for: SKI, SLED, SKATE, SNOW ANGELS, SNOW, SNOWBALLS, SNOW FORT, SNOWMAN, HOCKEY, ICE COLD, ICE FISHING, TOBOGGAN.

```
S N O W I C E C O L D I
S S N E P M O N W M S C
L K O T L Y E K C O H E
E A I O Y S Y A T M S F
D T A B M L N E R N N I
V E A O O E I S O A O S
W G M G A G D W F I W H
L C O G N N M S W O B I
C Y N A A A I C O I A N
F R O N N W A O N P L G
O A F R E O M R S N L L
L R N I Z N T O R C S I
O N E S S S O P G E A P
A B S P L N A M W O N S
```

Bookmarks!

Grandfather Alden's old house in Michigan is full of beautiful rooms. But no room is more exciting than the library. It is filled with old books about adventure, mystery, romance, and history.

Five books have disappeared from the library. The kids think they might be in the parlor. Can you find them? Circle each book when you discover it.

A Diamond a Dozen!

Emily's diary sends the Aldens on a search for a real diamond ring. There are twelve rings in this picture, but only one has a real diamond. Can you guess which one it is? It's different from the rest.

The Joke's on You!

Emily's diary is filled with riddles and jokes. That makes Benny very happy! Nobody likes a joke better than Benny Alden.

Here are some of the oldest (and silliest) jokes in the world. Can you match the riddle to its punch line?

A. When can five big men stand under a tiny umbrella and not get wet?
B. Waiter! What is this fly doing in my soup?
C. How do you catch a squirrel?
D. What has four wheels and flies?
E. What is green and can leap tall buildings in a single bound?

1. Climb a tree and act like a nut.
2. A garbage truck.
3. When it is not raining!
4. Super Pickle.
5. I think it's doing the backstroke, sir.

Photographic Memory!

Violet spotted an old camera in a neighborhood pawnshop. But now she can't remember where in the shop it was. How good is your memory?

Color in this picture any way you'd like. Try to remember everything you can. Then turn the page and see how well your memory works!

Photographic Memory Questions

Circle the picture in each row that is exactly the same as the one in the picture you just colored.

Amazing Things to Make and Do!

When the Aldens lived in their little red boxcar, they had no money. They had to make everything they needed. Now that the kids live with their grandfather, they can buy almost anything they want. But the Aldens still remember how much fun it is to use something you've made yourself, or to eat a home-baked snack.

Now Henry, Jessie, Violet, and Benny want *you* to join in the fun. They've gathered some of their favorite recipes and craft ideas and written them down just for you!

Why not give them a try?

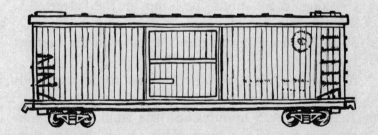

Not from the Bakery Window!

Henry's favorite blueberry muffins come straight from your oven. Ask an adult to help you make them, though!

You will need: 2 cups flour, 4 teaspoons baking powder, 1/2 teaspoon salt, 1/4 cup sugar, 1 egg beaten, 1/4 cup of melted margarine, 1 cup milk, 1 cup blueberries (if you don't like blueberries, try raisins instead).

Here's what you do:
1. Ask an adult to preheat your oven to 400 degrees.
2. Mix the dry ingredients together in one bowl. Mix the wet ingredients in another bowl.
3. Use a mixing spoon to combine the ingredients in the two bowls. Do not mix the ingredients for too long (there should be lumps in the batter).
4. Stir in the blueberries.
5. Fill greased muffin tins 3/4 full with the muffin batter.
6. Ask an adult to put the muffins in the oven and bake for 25 minutes.
7. After the 25 minutes, ask the adult to take the muffins out of the oven. Wait for the muffins to cool.
Makes 12–15 muffins

Paper Periscope

The Boxcar Children sometimes spy on people to solve their mysteries. One of their best spy tools is this periscope. It allows the Aldens to see things that are not in their direct line of vision.

You will need: 2 half-gallon milk or juice cartons, scissors, 2 small mirrors, masking tape.

Here's what you do:
1. Ask an adult to help you cut the tops off of the milk or juice cartons.
2. Ask the same adult to help you cut a viewing square two inches wide and one inch high, one inch from the bottom of each carton. Cut only one viewing hole in each carton.
3. Tape the mirrors to the bottom and side of each carton at a 45° angle. (See drawing.)
4. Use the masking tape to connect the cartons together at their open ends. Tape the cartons so that the viewing holes are at opposite ends and opposite sides of the periscope.
5. Now you are ready to spy! Stand near something that is taller than you but low enough so the top of your periscope sticks up over it. (A fence is a good object to stand behind.) Look through the bottom opening of your periscope, and you will see what's going on over the fence!

Peppy Peppermint Chocolate!

What goes better with muffins than a mug of hot chocolate? Here's Jessie's recipe for hot chocolate with a peppermint twist!

You will need: 1 cup milk, 1 teaspoon chocolate syrup, and a peppermint stick.

Here's what you do: Combine the milk and chocolate in a pot. Ask an adult to warm the chocolate milk for you. Then ask the adult to pour the warm chocolate milk into a mug for you. Place the peppermint stick in the mug. Then use the peppermint stick as a straw to drink your hot chocolate. (Be patient. A few strong sips and that peppermint stick will hollow itself out.)

A Penny for the Page

Emily's diary is so fascinating, the Boxcar Children don't want to miss a single word! So they made this cool bookmark to make sure they keep their place. The best part is it doesn't cost much to make — just two cents!

You will need: rubber cement, a large paper clip, two pennies.

Here's what you do:
1. Put a dab of the rubber cement on the center of one of the pennies.
2. Glue the penny to the end of the paper clip that has one loop.
3. Put another dab of rubber cement on the second penny.
4. Glue the second penny to the paper clip so that the two pennies sandwich the paper clip. Allow the glue to dry completely.
5. To use your paper clip bookmark, slide the page of your book into the paper clip.

Answers

It's a Mystery:

Outdoor Fun:

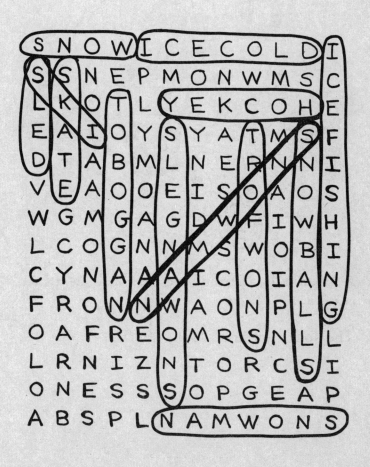

Bookmarks:

A Diamond a Dozen!: Number nine is the real diamond ring.

The Joke's on You!: A3, B5, C1, D2, E4

Photographic Memory: